# ART HEISTS AND HAIRBALLS

## Spy Kitty in the City

**BAILEY BOOTH**

All Rights Reserved.

Copyright © 2021 Bailey Booth. All Rights Reserved. This is a work of fiction. All characters appearing in this work are fictitious. Any resemblance to real persons, living or dead, is purely coincidental. No part of this publication may be reproduced in any manner without the express written consent of the publisher, except in the case of brief excerpts in critical reviews or articles. All inquiries should be addressed to hibailey@baileyboothbooks.com

Booth, Bailey. Art Heists and Hairballs (Spy Kitty in the City)

Cover design by Molly Burton of Cozy Cover Designs

# CHAPTER ONE

Hi, I'm Addie Dawson, and pulling up to Helping Paws Animal Shelter always filled me with trepidation. Not the *I hate my job* variety. Just the opposite. I loved my job, but I wished there wasn't any reason for me to have it. The sinking feeling was solely associated with the fact I never knew what might wait for me when I got there.

This was one of those mornings.

My coffee soured in my belly when I spotted the box sitting by the door. Not even a travel crate. A cardboard box. Ugh.

We marched to the beat of our own drums in Harmony, New Hampshire. That was why I felt at home here. So there was an outside chance we'd received a middle-of-the-night delivery.

But I knew better.

I said a quick prayer to Saint Francis of Assisi and climbed out of the car. He was the patron saint of animals, and I had his metaphorical number on speed dial.

"Hey, buddy," I said as I lowered myself to the pavement beside the box. Dampness immediately seeped through my leggings. The responding yowl sounded an awful lot like *help*! Definitely a cat, but when they were scared, animals all spoke the same language. I needed to gain its trust in a hurry. "I know you'll find this hard to believe, but things will only get better from here on out. My name's Addie, and you're at Helping Paws. You're safe here. You'll be warm, fed, and loved and then I'll find you an awesome forever home."

I was rewarded with another loud meow and some scratching in response. Good. I liked them feisty.

"This isn't my first rodeo, so I'll bring you inside before I let you out." I fully expected that protest when I lifted the box. The only thing more heart-breaking than finding an animal waiting for me in the parking lot was having them escape before we even got in the door. This was New Hampshire, and we had some serious wildlife waiting in the woods behind the shelter for that kind of opportunity.

Kicking the door closed behind me, I swiped the

light switch with my elbow. I'd done this too many times. The animals who called Helping Paws home greeted me.

"Good morning! We have someone new. I'll be getting them settled and Brooke and Casey will be here soon to help me get everyone fed." People thought I was crazy for telling the animals everything I planned to do, but I liked to think they understood me. Even if they didn't know the words, they definitely understood intent and goodwill.

My efforts were met with another yowl I hoisted the box onto the table. Whoever was inside was pretty heavy, which I hoped was a good sign. A paw poked through the drooping slit that was supposed to be an airhole. I hit speed dial to Saint Francis one more time, hoping Brooke would be able to handle whoever I found inside when she arrived. She was studying to be a vet, and what she didn't have in certifications she made up for with some seriously on-point instincts. Although my employees were always quick to suggest we call Dr. Oliver, the good-looking recent veterinarian grad that volunteered time at the shelter when he could.

The yowls from the box became more urgent, almost human sounding.

"You're almost out, I promise." I put on my gloves

before slitting the duct tape that held the soggy cardboard together.

I was greeted by a plump, frowning cat. Ears back, eyes full of rage. And a hiss.

"I like that you've got some fight in you after a rough night. You're safe here." I didn't attempt to pick up the cat yet. I liked having eyeballs too much to even thinking about handling an angry animal. "Newcomers get wet food. It's a luxury I can't give you every day, but we'll make sure you're comfortable here until we can find you a home."

The newest resident of Helping Paws was a black cat, and they were notoriously hard to adopt. We were a no-kill shelter, but each long-term resident meant that we wouldn't have the room to help someone else.

I'd do everything in my power to find this cat a new home. Just like I did for everyone who came through our doors.

Placing the food and water on the table, I smiled at the cat, who'd taken the first opportunity of freedom to clean themself. Besides some muddy paws, this cat appeared to be in good shape. Saint Francis was reading his text messages today.

The cat looked me square in the eye. "I need your help."

"Of course you do."

Wait a minute, what?

I turned to the door, but no one was there. It was just me and the shelter animals. I looked at the cat again. "What did you say?"

I was treated to one of those exasperated looks that only a cat could give. "I need help. I've been catnapped."

"Good morning!" Casey called out as she walked in with Brooke. The animals went wild in response to her voice. There was something about the way she talked to them that made them all fall in love with her. When she wasn't working at the shelter, she was a YouTube influencer, so we played her videos for the animals when we needed to soothe them. "We brought oatmeal breakfast cookies."

"Are you actually going to eat them this time?" Casey loved to cook, but she frequently had a first date on the horizon, which meant Brooke and I reaped the benefits of her hobby. I didn't mind. My idea of a perfect Friday night was sitting in front of the TV watching the weekly marathon of my favorite cooking show, Parking Lot Potluck, and eating food someone else made.

"It's Friday, so it means I've got to fit into Lucky." It was the name of her little black dress that never disappointed.

The ladies approached the table and frowned.

"I see we have someone new." Brooke swallowed a mouthful of cookie and squinted to inspect the cat. "Did the cat come in this box or is this a *if it fits I sits* situation?"

"I was catnapped!" The cat protested again. The voice had a hint of an older female, one who'd had a pack-a-day habit and had seen some *things*. "I need your help!"

The ladies cooed over the cat, offering a hand to sniff before scratching her head.

"Did you hear that?" I asked.

"Hear what?" Casey asked. "She's purring, so she's friendly."

"They found the spot." The cat grimaced. "I can't stop purring when someone finds the spot."

It was official. I'd lost my mind. "You don't notice anything unusual about her?"

"Not yet. She's beautiful and well fed," Brooke said. "And pretty trusting for someone...you never said if she came in this box."

"Yup. Found her waiting for me outside the door in a damp box."

The ladies groaned. We'd had many conversations addressing what we thought about anyone who could do such a thing to an animal and there was no need to revisit.

The cat pushed up to encourage more head rubs.

She hadn't gone for the food right away, which was odd. Most of our new residents were hungry. Maybe she had been catnapped, like she'd said.

Or the lady at the drive-up window put hallucinogens in my coffee.

"She wants something."

Brooke, Casey, and the cat glared at me when I said that.

"That totally came out wrong. Are you sure you don't notice anything strange?"

"She's in awfully good shape to come here in this ratty box. That doesn't make any sense." Brooke furrowed her brow. "Once we get everyone else fed, I'll give her an examination."

"What are you seeing, Addie?" Casey asked. "I haven't had my coffee yet. You need to spell it out."

Did I tell them?

"I've been catnapped," the cat said again. "You all seem very nice, but I want to go home."

Here goes nothing. "Does it sound like she's...talking?"

That was the look I expected.

"Nothing other than purrs."

"I swear I can understand her." Way to double down on the unbelievable.

Brooke and Casey side-eyed each other. "You do have a special touch with the new animals. You make them feel at home here," Casey finally said. "Maybe that's why you think she's talking."

"Okay, never mind then." I turned on my heel before they could see me turn red. "I'll get the kibble ready for the rest of the residents."

"Addie!" Brooke called me back. "What did she say?"

I swallowed hard. It was almost impossible to find good, loyal employees who worked as hard as Brooke and Casey. They were students at Harmony Community College, and they wouldn't be with me forever. Brooke would be a doctor, and Casey had plans for online world domination.

"She says she's been catnapped."

Their lips quivered, and I wasn't sure if they wanted to laugh or cry. I put my hand on the cat's head, loving the little internal motor of approval. I needed it.

"There are people who can communicate with animals," Brooke said. "We're learning about it in school. It's new science, and controversial, because" —she gestured at me and the cat— "but my question is, why would you be able to understand this cat, and none of the others here?"

"Just lucky, I guess?" Maybe I hadn't lost it after all. "Maybe I should stick with her and see what else she says."

The ladies hung up their coats, put on their aprons and got to work, and I stayed with our newest resident. She watched my every move.

I put my hands on my hips. I spent plenty of time talking to animals, but the conversations had always been one-sided. Now that there were other humans here, I was a self-conscious about continuing the conversation. "Am I the only one you can talk to?"

"*I* can talk to everyone. So far, *you're* the only one who's understood *me*." The cat stood, stretched, and carefully stepped over the drooping side of the box. "Do you have any tuna?"

"Okay, so you're not a stray." Besides the muddy paws, my new friend had a shiny, thick coat, white legs that made it look like she was wearing pants, and a pudgy belly.

She groaned. "I told you, I was catnapped."

"What happened?" I had to admit, it was amazing to get the story of why she'd been dropped off here. Usually we were left guessing.

"I witnessed a crime." The cat walked toward me, stopping at the edge of the table. Her yellow gaze captivated me. "I chased the robbers, but I lost them. I tried to find my way back to the gallery, but there were so many scents!"

Gallery. Interesting. Not home. She wore a pink

collar, but there was no pendant sharing her information. I hoped she had a chip.

"There was a box outside, and some food in there. I was starving. The next thing I knew, I woke up and the box was sealed. Now I'm here."

"I'm food motivated too. What's your name?"

She steeled herself. "Persephone."

"Nice to meet you, Persephone." I looked toward the kennel area. Brooke and Casey were busy feeding and greeting our residents. They were soaking up dog kisses and cat rubs and weren't paying us any mind. Persephone drank her water, but she wasn't touching the food. "Do you know where you live? Or your owners' names?"

The cat gave me a look.

"Silly me. No one owns you. What can you tell me about the people who feed and take care of you?"

"My person is called Margaret, and she owns the Galerie Bellamy. She must be devastated about the missing painting. And of course, me."

Oh. Galerie Bellamy had been all over the internet. A priceless painting had been stolen in the middle of the night last week. It was a Bournaise, a trendy "new" painter, though he hadn't lived to enjoy his fifteen minutes of fame. The stories online had been pretty juicy, claiming the owner of the gallery had been the lover of the artist.

Last I read, they had no leads on who took the painting.

There was a huge reward for information leading to the recovery of the Bournaise. Money that would go a long way in helping the residents of Helping Paws who didn't have a voice. With Persephone's help, I might be able to claim it.

# CHAPTER TWO

"Are you coming out with us tonight, Addie?" Brooke asked.

"I thought Casey had a date."

She rolled her eyes. "He canceled. I need to stop swiping on this stupid site."

"Maybe we should set you up with Doctor Oliver." I waggled my brows.

"We could, but he's only got eyes for the animals."

"And Addie," Brooke added, and I groaned. "Don't lie, the two of you have shared some longing looks that have nothing to do with veterinary business."

"I can't date him. If it goes bad, we'll have no one to help with the animals."

"So are you coming with us?" Brooke waggled her brows.

"Add tonight to my ever-growing collection of rainchecks."

Casey waved her hand and tossed her apron into the hamper. "We're never getting her to go out after work. I swear, when I get my Boost Your Self-Confidence course finished, I'm giving you a free pass."

"My confidence is fine. You don't want an old lady hanging around with you." At thirty-two, I was ten years older than my coworkers. We had a ton of fun at work, but I was their boss, and there were supposed to be boundaries. Which was why all I could share with the adorable doctor was those looks. The funny thing was, I hated rules. I ditched my brokerage job for that reason. But now that I was in charge, rules sometimes came in handy. "Persephone told me who her owner is, and I want to see if I can contact her."

"Persephone?" Casey raised a brow. "Purr-sephone? Whoever named her has a sense of humor."

"And they're probably missing her."

"That's a valid reason to bail. You'll come out with us next weekend, then?" Brooke bounced on her toes, giving me her most hopeful look.

"I came home to New Hampshire to embrace my socially awkward self. After working all week, I'm super happy to veg out in front of my cooking shows."

"You don't even cook."

"I like to eat." I had a little bit of a takeout problem. I reframed it: I support local businesses.

"You know where to find us if you change your mind. Or if Persephone has more to say." Brooke winked at me on her way out the door. Casey waved and followed.

Tonight, I had a date with a cat.

I knew better than to show up empty handed. After a quick trip to the supermarket to stock up on solid tuna in oil, I returned to Helping Paws. This would be easier if I could bring Persephone home as a foster, but I lived in the in-law apartment above my sister's garage, and in exchange for jaw-droppingly cheap rent, she forbade me from bringing any animals home with me. She insisted her kids were allergic—to everything—but I had a feeling it was her way of making sure I didn't get comfortable up there.

The crack of the can got a few curious meows from our other feline residents. Persephone's new travel case was still sitting on the front table. I didn't see the point in getting her acclimated since I'd most likely be bringing her home over the weekend.

"Hope you're good with sharing," I said when I opened the door to the kennel.

Persephone rubbed against my hand. I probably

smelled like the good stuff. "As long as you got enough for everyone."

"Can you understand what they say?"

"Of course I can."

"Tell me everything." Having a translator would be amazing, and I had to make use of my short time with Persephone. She had a home, and it was my job to reunite her with it.

"The one next to Harriet wants to be moved. Says she snores. Marcy, at the end, is afraid of the dark."

"Oh. I'll find a nightlight." And do a little rearranging before I left for the night.

Maybe I could make a deal with Persephone's person to have her come visit every once in a while. Like a cat consultant.

I paced the waiting area of the shelter as Persephone and the others enjoyed their meals.

I hated making phone calls, but calling the gallery cranked my anxiety to eleven. Usually I was excited to reunite a pet with their human, but Persephone came in with no tags, in a soggy box. What if she'd wound up here on purpose? I'd use the same criteria I used to evaluate potential adopters to make sure I was returning her to a safe, loving home.

Maybe Persephone knew who took the painting... visions of reward money were definitely dancing in my head. That money could do so many good things for the shelter. I might have borrowed against it when I went on my tuna shopping spree.

Gourmet meals weren't a part of the Helping Paws' budget.

"Thank you," she said as she licked her paw after she emptied the bowl. "Haven't had a meal like that in...ages."

From the looks of her tummy, that was an exaggeration. We'd thought she might be pregnant until Brooke examined her. But I wasn't one to food shame. I thoroughly enjoyed my treats too.

"Can you tell me anything else about the stolen painting?" I asked.

She stopped licking. "It belongs to Margaret, and they took it when she was sleeping."

That was an odd detail. "Does Margaret live at the gallery?"

I'd snuck in as much research about Galerie Bellamy as I could during the day. The owner's name was indeed Margaret, and at the time of the theft, she had been putting together an exhibit of Bournaise paintings, set to open next weekend. There was so much buzz around the exhibit she had to sell advance tickets.

"Yes. Her house is upstairs. The gallery is downstairs."

"And you go back and forth?" I'd think there were

separate doors, like my apartment was separate from my sister's house.

"I like the gallery. There's a spot in the window that's good for napping."

"Did you see who took the painting?" My imagination had been running wild all day, picturing skinny dudes wearing all black moving soundlessly through the gallery. Using acrobatics to dodge an intricate tangle of security lasers.

And apprehending them with my trusty sidekick, Persephone.

But there were so many questions, like how did they get in? The articles I read mentioned there was no forced entry. And how and why did Persephone wind up in another state?

"Two humans," she said.

I groaned but reminded myself to be patient. She was a cat. And all of this could be a figment of my imagination.

That was another reason the phone call gave me the heebie-jeebies.

Persephone huffed. "They smelled like dead flowers."

"Like perfume?" I was dealing with a cat, and I had to work with what she could give me. "Have you ever smelled that before?"

"All the time."

This reward money could be a slam dunk, if Persephone could be trusted. "Could you tell who it was?"

What was I going to do? Bring her in front of a lineup and let her sniff her fill?

"Don't know. A lot of people come in and out of the gallery. Scents linger. But this one, I've smelled a lot."

She might think all humans smelled like that, or maybe she was picking up on Margaret's perfume. I wished there was another cat here I could talk to, so I could get more insight on how this all worked.

"Do I have a scent?"

Her eyes brightened. "You smell like treats."

"What kind of treats?"

"Sweet ones."

The cookies Casey had brought in. They were delicious and easy to pop in my mouth in between all the tasks we needed to do each day to keep the shelter running smoothly.

So the scent wasn't a smoking gun, but I wasn't giving up yet. I'd probably only have one chance to talk to Margaret, so I needed to be prepared.

"What happened after the humans took the painting?"

"I followed them. They had no right to take it!" Persephone rose and stretched, indignance oozing out of every pore. "They brought it through an alley, onto the street, and loaded it into a car."

If Persephone couldn't describe a person to me, she'd never be able to give me critical details on the getaway vehicle, like a license plate number. But that was still pretty good.

"Then what happened?"

"They almost ran me over." She huffed. "I chased them as long as I could. I'm not a kitten anymore, and I lost them."

"Why didn't you go back to the gallery?" I asked. Persephone seemed like a homebody.

"I wanted to find the car. Margaret's painting. Those humans can't get away with this." She lay down in front of me. "But I couldn't find them, so I tried to go home."

I wondered how many other animals in my care had stories like this. That they were trying to do a good thing for their human, and it went horribly wrong.

"How did you wind up in the box?"

"I made it back home to the alley. There was a box out there, and it had a treat in it. I thought maybe Margaret had left it for me. I don't remember anything else that happened until I woke up and couldn't get out of the box."

Someone had put catnip in that box. Cats passed

out if they ate it. Which made me think someone wanted Persephone…gone. A chill ran down my spine.

From Persephone's account, whoever took the painting was familiar with Margaret. And they took her cat away from her.

Why?

Maybe I should've spent my weekends watching crime shows instead of Parking Lot Potluck.

"You're really far from the gallery." That didn't deliver the shock value I was hoping for. Cats probably didn't measure things like distance, or time, like we did. "Did you smell anything on the way here?"

"Chemicals," she said.

"Do you know what kind?"

"No." She curled her paws in front of her, and yawned. She'd been through a lot and had to be exhausted. The clock was ticking on my investigation.

"I can call Margaret and tell her you're here." I ran my hand over her back. "Do you want to go home?"

It didn't sound like she'd had a bad life, but someone had put her in a box and brought her here for a reason.

"I like Margaret, yes. But I also like talking to you," she said.

"I like talking to you too." But I couldn't get attached. "Tell me about Margaret."

"She has a silly nickname for me. So unsophisticated."

"What is it?"

"I'd rather not share that information." If a cat could blush, Persephone would be bright pink.

"C'mon, tell me." I picked up my phone and swiped to the page I already had open with the gallery phone number. "Once I talk to Margaret, she'll probably say it."

She made a sound that was supposed to be a growl, but it was more like a moan.

"I'll probably make up my own nickname for you eventually."

She groaned. "Fine. She calls me Purry Pants. Because my back legs are a different color."

"It's cute." Oh, that was a look. "I promise I'll never call you that."

The phone was still in my hand, with the gallery number on the screen, and I held my breath as I hit send.

"Galerie Bellamy. Margaret speaking." Her voice had a slight shake to it. Thanks to my research, I had the unfair advantage of knowing a few things about Margaret, sight unseen. She was seventy years old and had recently returned to Boston after living in France for most of her adult life. She came from old money that had fizzled out in the last generation or so. The articles described her as colorful and eccentric.

"Hi, Margaret. My name is Addie Dawson. I think I might have your cat."

"Purry Pants?" I stifled a laugh at her exclamation. Persephone huffed and turned away from me. "Where did you find her? She's been missing since the night of...the break-in. I'm not sure if you've heard, my gallery was broken into."

"I'm very sorry for your loss." I groaned. A painting was missing, no one died. "Can you tell me a few things about your cat to make sure we don't have a case of mistaken identity?"

"Did you get my phone number from her tag?"

Interesting. "She came in without a tag. Would you like to come and see if she's your cat?"

"Yes, of course." There was a long pause. "How did you know she was my cat if she didn't have a tag?"

"She matched the description from one of the news stories about the break-in." I hadn't read a story that mentioned the cat, but it didn't mean they didn't exist.

"I don't think I...oh, it must've been Nicole, my niece, who mentioned Purry. She's been so helpful since the incident." She sighed. I couldn't blame her for being rattled. "Where is she?"

"At Helping Paws Animal Shelter in Harmony, New Hampshire."

"Oh, dear. That's so far. I'm not sure I can make it there. I'm reluctant to leave the gallery, in case the thieves come back for more. Maybe I could send my niece."

"I'd rather match the owner with the lost pet." And I wanted to see Margaret interact with Persephone in person. Persephone had said I was the first to understand her, but maybe Margaret would know something was different about her pet.

And I wanted to put together what I'd learned from Persephone and see if it matched anything that really happened. Not only for the reward money. Margaret sounded like a nice lady, and her cat obviously cared for her. They deserved justice.

"You're more than welcome to bring her here. The gallery will be open from ten to five, all weekend. I could meet with you after hours, so we could talk."

"I'll see you tomorrow night."

# CHAPTER THREE

There's a meme comparing the overhead street views of New York and Boston. The streets in New York are neatly organized in a grid. The streets of Boston look like someone dropped a bowl of spaghetti and was forever waiting for someone to pick it up. Add to that a subway strike and tourists walking into traffic on this summer evening, and I'd had to borrow a couple of Persephone's nine lives to get to Galerie Bellamy.

I was late, and being late gave me all the feels from my old brokerage job in Boston, where I always arrived five minutes late and totally flustered from traffic. I wasn't able to park near the gallery, and I was going to be sweaty by the time I met Margaret.

Looking at my phone and not where I was going, I slammed right into someone when I turned the corner so hard Persephone yowled from inside her carrier.

"I am so sorry." Even more mortifying, I'd slammed into a really cute guy. He was about my age, with dark wavy hair and dark-rimmed glasses. He was wearing a button-down shirt and a pair of jeans.

If Brooke and Casey were here, they'd definitely be flirting with him. But I turned multiple shades of red.

"It's all right. We all have places to go." He gave me a crooked grin and looked down at the carrier in my hand. "Taking your cat out for the night?"

"No. I'm bringing her back." That sounded ridiculous. "Is Galerie Bellamy on this street?"

His eyes widened. "Is that Persephone?"

"You know this cat?"

He crouched down and smiled when he got a good view of the carrier. "Yes, I do. And yeah, the gallery is in the middle of the block. You can't miss it. It's the only house in the middle of the high rises."

"Thank you." I sidestepped him, careful not to hit him in the head with the carrier. One assault was enough for the night.

His description was spot-on. One brownstone remained between the high-rises, a skinny Victorian holdout from a bygone era. Galerie Bellamy was dark, and the closed sign was on the glass door. I hoped I wasn't too late when I wrapped on the wooden door.

"Did you know that man?" I looked to either side, making sure no one was close enough to hear me talking to a cat.

"Yes. He comes to the gallery often."

"What does he smell like?"

"Chemicals."

My heart was pounding when Margaret appeared from a shadowy hallway. Persephone smelled chemicals the night of the heist. I might have just come face to face with the thief! What should I tell her?

She waved when she saw me, and her face lit up when she spotted the cat carrier in my hand. I liked her already. I'd seen her picture in the news stories, and she was a thin, stylish, older woman with thick gray hair down to her shoulders, where it flipped out a little, like she was still hanging onto her heyday style. Today she wore a black turtleneck with a statement necklace and wide-legged, patterned pants.

Way cooler than I could ever manage to pull off.

"You must be Addie. Please, come in," she said as she opened the door. "And that's my Purry Pants."

Persephone groaned from inside the carrier, but then meowed in response. Huh. I thought maybe she'd try to talk, but she was all cat in the presence of her person.

I crouched and opened the door to the carrier. Persephone strutted out and stretched. She looked around, and I wished I could ask her what she was looking for. She pushed up against Margaret's legs, and the older woman bent and scooped her up. "I'm so glad you made the time to meet with me."

"Of course. You have Purry Pants." She kissed her cat on the head. "Thank you so much for coming all this way. It will be a lot easier to get through this now that she's home."

"It's always good when we can reunite a pet with their family." I took a quick scan of the wall, looking for where the infamous painting might have been. But there weren't any holes in the display. She'd either rearranged things to disguise the loss, or the painting was never on display to begin with. "Any leads on the painting yet?"

"No, unfortunately. I haven't been as helpful as I should be, I'm afraid. Losing the painting was devasting."

"No one expects you to find the painting yourself." I wasn't sure what to say about the handsome man that fit the scent of the thief, according to the cat she was snuggling against her chest. I had to go slow with that information.

"Bellamy was my partner for many years. He considered me his muse." She chuckled sadly and looked into the distance, like she was indulging herself in a memory, then shook her head. "It's like losing him all over again."

"I'm sorry."

She leaned in close and whispered, "I've never told anyone this before, but I'm the subject of the painting that's missing. I should've never made it available for sale."

"Who's here?" A younger voice called from the hallway. A well put-together woman, the kind that always made me feel like a kid, even though I was in my thirties, appeared. Her face fell when she saw me standing there with Margaret. "Persephone's back, I see."

"Addie brought her here from a shelter in New Hampshire. Isn't that wonderful?"

"It certainly is. Now if we could have the same good fortune with the painting." The woman stuck her hand out to me. "I'm Nicole, Margaret's niece. I've been helping her with the exhibit, and now with the press in the aftermath of the theft."

"Nice to meet you." I drew my hand away, aware it was probably still sweaty. "Do you have any leads on who could've stolen the painting?"

Nicole drew back.

"Sorry if that was too forward. I've been reading

about the theft since I found out Persephone belonged here."

"We're working closely with the police, but we haven't been able to provide any credible suspects. It seems like my aunt left the door in the back unlocked." She gave her aunt a role-reversing look. "Too many people in and out of here. Sully, the handyman, he never sticks to any schedule."

"He cares way more about his sports teams than he does about art," Margaret interjected.

"Maybe someone hired him to do it for that reason."

"He's done everything I've asked him to. There's no reason to suspect him of wrongdoing." Margaret cuddled the cat closer to her.

Nicole turned to me. "I always tell her she's too trusting."

"Lies," Persephone said. "She tries to make Margaret feel old."

So this was uncomfortable.

"Whether the door was locked or not, nobody had any business helping themselves to a priceless work of art," I said. "Is there any way they could resell the painting on the black market? I've read that it's valued at a quarter of a million dollars."

"More than that." Nicole waved her hand. "I don't know anything about black markets. My business is real estate. That's why we're leaving the investigation to the experts."

Achievement unlocked: the first door slammed in my face in my fledging amateur investigator career.

"Nicole, take Addie's bag. She came a long way to bring Purry Pants back to me. The least we can do is offer her some tea and maybe some cake. I made a blueberry cake last night."

"Oh, I can't—"

"That sounds wonderful." I shrugged my purse off my shoulder and handed it to a scowling Nicole. She looked eager for me to hit the road, but I hadn't had anything since breakfast, and my stomach was rumbling.

Plus, I wanted to talk to Margaret alone.

"Would you show me around the gallery?" I asked when Nicole disappeared into a back room.

"I'd love to. We were almost done setting up the new exhibit for next weekend's party, but I may cancel it."

"Because of the theft?"

She nodded.

"No! That would be a shame." The thief had already taken enough from this woman.

Margaret gave Persephone a kiss on the head then set her down. "I'm not sure I want to share Bellamy's work with the world anymore. If he'd lived to see this interest in his art, he would've hated it. His work was in response to the culture he wanted to get away from. He probably would've stolen his own painting."

I laughed. "I would've liked Bellamy a lot."

"Every day with him took my breath away. I never knew what to expect." Her eyes shone with emotion. "My life isn't the same without him."

"I'm really glad I was able to bring Persephone back to you. That must make things a little easier."

"It does. She's good company." Margaret furrowed her brow. "How did you know to bring her here if her tag was missing?"

I stepped closer and waited for the telltale sounds of cabinets being opened to make sure Nicole was distracted. "Has your cat ever, uh, talked to you?"

Margaret pursed her lips, blinking. "She's quite a vocal cat. Especially around mealtime."

I shook my head. "I mean, actually spoken?" My heart pounded. Margaret seemed to have had an avant-garde past—but this was pretty farfetched. "I didn't believe my ears at first either, but how else would I know she's your cat?"

"She was in the press—"

"I said that because I was afraid to tell you that I can talk to your cat." Another glance at the hallway to make sure the coast was still clear. "She followed the thieves. She knows who took your painting."

"There must be some explanation."

"Can I prove it to you? Maybe she can tell me which window she likes to nap in?"

"The one near the door," Persephone said. "It's got enough room to get comfy."

I pointed to it, and Margaret's lips parted.

The clicking of heels signaled Nicole was back, with a cup of tea in each hand. The younger woman looked like she was much more accustomed to people waiting on her than the other way around.

"Maybe we should sit," Margaret suggested and turned to Nicole. "Addie might know who took the painting,"

Nicole narrowed her eyes at me.

"I wouldn't go that far." I followed them into a room that had the kitchen essentials, but also a massive table in the middle, and a few sculptures positioned on it like someone was figuring out how to display them.

"We're reconsidering offering the reward money, if that's what you're after," Nicole said as she took her seat. "Selling the Bournaise was supposed to fund my aunt's retirement. She can't afford to give money away if she doesn't sell that painting."

"Certainly understandable." Something about Nicole was rubbing me the wrong way. She reminded me of someone who would've turned up their nose at me at a cocktail party at the brokerage firm I used to work at.

Persephone curled around my legs. "Two people took the painting," she said. She'd told me that at the shelter, too.

Which supported the Sully getting paid-off theory. I wondered if he was the guy I almost knocked over on the sidewalk. He did know Persephone, and according to her, he smelled the same…

"Was there anyone especially interested in the exhibit?" I asked. "Maybe someone who hasn't been around much since the theft?"

"We've already spoken to the police," Nicole reminded me, frowning from behind her teacup. "Perhaps you should contact them if you have information that could lead to an arrest?"

Margaret shook her head, like her niece embarrassed her. "A lot of people are excited about the exhibit, since Bellamy's other work has gained attention. I've had these paintings in my house since I moved back to the States, and I decided to make them available, with some encouragement."

"From the art teacher." Nicole rolled her eyes. "He spends an awful lot of time in a tiny gallery."

Margaret's face lit up. "Henry's fascinating. He's traveled to some of the same places that Bellamy and

I did. Even studied with Bellamy's protégé. We have a lot in common. I enjoy his company."

"Bet selling a Bournaise on the black market would pad his teacher's salary." Nicole waved off a piece of cake when Margaret offered. "You should've never given him the code to the gallery."

Oh. I hoped Henry had an alibi for the night. And that he wasn't working with Sully.

Poor Sully. I'd already totally framed him.

Margaret shrugged. "He likes to work here. It's impossible to sculpt in a tiny apartment."

I did not turn down Margaret's offer of cake.

"Henry's very talented," she said and motioned to the sculptures in progress on the table. "This is his work."

It didn't look like much now—white plaster, maybe, with some carvings. I nodded because I had no idea what to say.

"He may also be very opportunistic," Nicole said. "Do you have any proof he really studied with Bellamy's people? Like I said, my aunt is too trusting. Too bohemian."

"Too bad more people aren't like that." I popped a piece of blueberry cake into my mouth as Nicole glared at me. "Does anyone else have the code?"

"Nicole does," Persephone said. "She was meeting a man here. He stunk."

"No," Margaret said. "Just Henry."

Interesting that Persephone thought to include Nicole but Margaret didn't. Maybe because she was family, she felt it went without saying. But even though I lived above my sister's garage, she didn't give me a key to her house.

"Is there anyone interested in this house? It seems to be an anomaly, a single-family house in the middle of so many high rises." I turned to Nicole. "You said you were in real estate, correct?"

"The house been in the family for generations," Margaret said. "But I have had some offers to sell. Nicole thinks I'm crazy to hold onto it."

"They're willing to pay well above market value, and market value is pretty impressive. The offer might not last forever." Nicole gave me a knowing smile. It made me shudder. "You could have a nice gallery down the Cape, or maybe in Florida."

"With the old people." Margaret groaned. "The minute I hand over the deed, they'll tear the place down and put up a high rise in its place. As soon as I'm gone, I'm sure the family will sell. But there's history here. I'd like to hold onto the legacy a little while longer."

Nicole put her hand over Margaret's. "I'd love to stay and chat more, but I have dinner reservations.

Addie, thank you so much for bringing my aunt's cat back. It was a very kind thing to do."

She rose from the table and put her coat over her arm before walking out the back door.

"I don't like her," Persephone said as she jumped into my lap. "She underestimates Margaret."

Margaret sighed when the door closed. "She always says I work too hard. Wants me to relax." She laughed sharply. "I'm seventy, I'm not dead. Having the gallery in the city is my connection to the art community."

"When does the exhibit open? *If* you do it."

"We planned to have the opening party next Saturday night. I'm not ready to retire, but I wonder if Nicole is right. If it is time for me to sell this house. I miss France, and my community there." With worry furrowing her brow, she did look older. Unsure. There was no doubt the theft had her rattled.

"Even if you decide to sell, I think you should still have the party. Think of it as a way to celebrate Bellamy. If you sell any of his work, and it sounds like you will, you can spend it on your terms."

"True…"

"I'd love to come, if that's possible. Maybe I could work with Persephone, and she could scent the person who took the painting. The perp might show up as part of their cover, or they could be scoping out their next target."

Margaret gasped. "It would break my heart if more of Bellamy's work was stolen."

"It won't be." Now I was making promises I couldn't keep. "We might get information the police would overlook and help them with the investigation."

"It's worth a try." Her face brightened and she reached over and patted Persephone's head. "Are you able to talk to other animals?"

"No. Can't lie, I questioned my sanity when it happened. But everything she told me led me to you. Your cat might be able to help you get your painting back."

"What do I wear to an art exhibit opening?" I'd donated all my old corporate clothes the minute I quit my soulless brokerage gig. Margaret was cool. I liked to think I was too, but I had a different aesthetic. "An animal has probably peed on every top I own."

"You should borrow Lucky. She's never failed me," Casey said.

"That's not the kind of luck I'm hoping for. Plus I'm..."—I motioned to the space between the top of my head and the top of hers, which I could barely reach—"shorter and...rounder than you."

"The dress has good mojo." She waggled her eyebrows at me. "Maybe you'll meet someone at the party."

I groaned. "That's not why I'm going."

"How are you going to pull this off?" Brooke asked. "It's not like you can hang out in the corner with a cocktail and have a casual conversation with Persephone while the party goes on around you."

"I'm playing it by ear." I shrugged. "I'm hoping that I'll be able to talk to a few people and maybe compare notes with Persephone afterward."

"How did Margaret react when you told her you could talk to her cat?" The ladies still weren't sold on the talking cat angle. Not that I could blame them.

I chuckled. "Similar to you, until I told her where Persephone liked to take naps. But then her niece showed up, and we didn't have a chance to talk about it again."

Brooke waggled her eyebrows. "I've been reading about the theft since you told us who Persephone belonged to. It sounds like she had a sizzling hot affair with a European artist."

"It sounds like more than that. She said she was his muse."

Casey put her hand over her heart. "That's so romantic. I would love it if someone called me their muse."

Brooke's face brightened. "Maybe we should all go to the party. There have got to be some single artists there. Addie won't take advantage."

Casey shook her head. "Those creative guys

always break your heart in the worst way. It's best to give them a wide berth."

"It's an art opening, not speed dating." I laughed and picked up the phone. "Helping Paws Animal Shelter."

"Hi, can I speak to Addie, please?" a deep male voice asked. Dare I say, a sexy voice.

"Speaking."

"My name is Henry Becket. I'm a patron of Galerie Bellamy, and I think I might have run into you and Persephone on Saturday night."

My mouth dropped. I'd pictured Henry as older and maybe as smelling like pipe smoke. Not the hot guy from the sidewalk. Who smelled like the thief.

"Hi," I squeaked.

"I was wondering if you'd be interested in talking about Bournaise? I've been studying his work for quite some time, and Margaret thinks you might have some information about the theft."

"What did she say?" I turned away from my curious audience before they could see that my cheeks pinked.

"That you had some sharp investigative skills that helped you bring her cat home safely."

"I'll be at the party on Saturday night."

"Would you be able to meet before then? You must be busy, but maybe we could go look at some art?"

"At Margaret's gallery?"

"Actually, I was thinking of the ICA. They have a new exhibit I've been interested in checking out. One of Bellamy's contemporaries. Not sure you're familiar with his work, but there's a reason people are finally paying attention."

The museum sounded safe. I couldn't be swayed because he was attractive. Persephone and Nicole had pointed a pretty credible finger in Henry's direction when it came to suspects. It was probably the only thing they agreed on.

I reminded myself what the reward money could do for the shelter.

I wished I could bring Persephone as an emotional support cat. My partner in fighting crime.

"What night would you like to meet?" I asked.

The ladies' mouths gaped. They thought this was a date.

"They're open late on Thursday. Does that work for you?"

"It does." A smile spread across my face.

"Is there a better number to reach you at?"

I gave him my cell number. Casey and Brooke

came closer, trying to figure out who I was talking to. "See you Thursday."

Casey put her hands on her hips and blocked me from coming out from behind the desk. "Addie. Do you have a date?"

"Not exactly." The smile got bigger. "I'm meeting with one of Margaret's patrons to talk about the missing painting."

"Who is it?" Brooke asked. "And how did he get the shelter number?"

"Come on, let's get back to work and I'll tell you."

I motioned for them to follow me to the kennels. The dogs knew it was playtime and they were headed to the backyard while we cleaned out their area. Not everyone was excited. Poor old Rufus had been our longest resident. His muzzle had gone completely gray while he stayed with us. He didn't love playing with the younger dogs, and I always let him curl up under my desk. There was a blanket and an old teddy bear that he loved to snuggle with waiting for him there.

"We have three appointments for adoptions tomorrow. Beasley, Champ, and Meow Meow, so we have to get everything ready for them."

"You can't change the subject like that. Tell us about your date."

"It's not a date." Although my burning cheeks said

otherwise. "His name's Henry and he's an art teacher."

"In Boston?"

"I assume so."

"Is he coming here?" Brooke asked.

"I'm meeting him at the ICA."

Casey's eyebrows disappeared into her bangs. "You're going to Boston three times in one week? And your cheeks are pink. This is a date."

"I'm interested in meeting him. Again."

"Again?"

"Yeah, I ran into him quickly when I brought Persephone back." No need to tell them I meant that literally. "He might know something about the missing painting."

"Is he cute?" Casey asked.

"Very."

"And this isn't a date?"

"He studied under Bellamy, and he spends a lot of time at the gallery." I chewed my lip. "Margaret's niece thinks he might be a suspect."

The girls gasped.

"Why does she think that?" Casey was always calm when Brooke and I tended to freak out.

"There was no sign of forced entry, and Henry has the code to the gallery. So Nicole, that's the niece, thinks he might have helped himself." I shrugged. "Teachers don't make a lot of money, so—"

Brooke held up her hands. "He could be danger-ous. I never thought I'd hear myself say this, but there's no way you can go on this date."

"There are other suspects. Like Sully, the handy-man. He's got a key too." Maybe I needed to figure out a way to talk to him. He'd have a perspective no one else would.

"But *he* didn't ask you on a date."

"It's not a date."

"Wait. Hear me out." Casey tapped her finger against her chin. "Maybe Henry can understand Persephone too, and he's the one who brought her all the way out here. The cat's back, and his secret is in jeopardy. Brooke's right. You can't go on this date."

"We're meeting in a totally public place." My phone dinged in my pocket. I had a text from an unknown Boston number with an image attached. "Oh, my goodness."

"What?"

*Looking forward to meeting you* was the message, accompanied by a photo. *In case you didn't remember me.* I handed the phone to my coworkers. Their eyes widened as they examined exhibit one.

"Henry is a total hottie." Brooke whistled low as she handed the phone back to me.

"Maybe I shouldn't go."

"Oh, you're totally going." Casey took the phone from me one more time to check out Henry the hottie.

I snatched the phone. "Minutes ago, you thought he was a serial killer."

"Art thief. Totally different story." She pushed against Brooke's shoulder. "We should go too."

"No."

She waved her hand. "You'll never see us. Think of us as your invisible wing women. We'll just be in the museum, immersing ourselves in art, and if gives you any hints he's got a history of doing crimes, text us, and we'll come to your rescue."

"Neither of you are very good at blending into the background." But it would be nice to have someone there, in case they were right, and Henry was dangerous.

"If we go with you, you don't have to drive into the city," Brooke added.

My hatred of city driving was no secret.

"We can be on the lookout for clues, too." Casey picked up a dog that had been bouncing at her feet. "I've never solved a crime before, but given the right information, I might be good at it."

I laughed. "Or you don't want to work on your new course."

She sighed as she put the dog down. "I'm in some serious need of inspiration. If I can use you as a case study on how to gain confidence in the places you least expect it.... That's it! That's my new course. See? You're my inspiration, Addie. You can't let me down."

# CHAPTER FIVE

Henry the Hottie waited for me in the lobby of the ICA, with his hands in the pockets of his khakis. His dark wavy hair was probably a week overdue for a cut, and his dark-rimmed glasses screamed academic chic.

And I had to remind myself this was not a date.

It took everything I had not to tuck tail and run back to the car. Like Brooke and Casey would let me. I had nothing to be nervous about—unless Nicole was right, and Henry had helped himself to the Bournaise.

First, I talked to a cat. Now I thought I was going to crack an art heist.

What even was my life?

His face lit up when he saw me. Brooke and Casey

had insisted on giving me a makeover before we left New Hampshire and I definitely wasn't feeling like myself. I waved and walked over to him.

My invisible wing women were already in the ticket line. Hopefully he didn't see them give me the thumbs up as I approached.

"Have you ever been here before?" he asked.

I shook my head. "I don't know much about art, but I do like looking at it."

"I can work with that." His smile shouldn't have made my heart flutter. The voice was enough of a distraction. "I spend my days trying to get bored teenagers excited about the classics. Someone who's interested? Piece of cake."

"Margaret told me you taught, but I assumed college."

"It's a private school, so funding to the arts hasn't been cut, yet, but the administrators have a very specific idea about culture. What will get the kids accepted into a top college. I wish they'd let me bring the students here, so they could appreciate work by people they might consider contemporaries, but if I want a paycheck, I have to teach their approved curriculum."

"Maybe you can sneak some of the modern stuff in," I suggested as we headed to the line.

"I do my best."

"A rulebreaker." I inwardly groaned. Obvious, much?

"Not exactly. But we should meet the students where they are, and then deepen their appreciation from there." Henry waved me off when I pulled out my wallet, which I would be eternally grateful for. I was footing the bill for Brooke and Casey's adventure tonight, taking yet another advance against my imaginary reward money.

"You work at an animal shelter?" he asked as we headed into the museum.

I nodded. "I've been there for almost ten years now. It's rewarding but heartbreaking work, even though Helping Paws is a no-kill shelter."

"I'd love to get a dog, but I'm not home much, and it wouldn't be fair to him."

"We're always looking for volunteers." Good move, inviting a suspected thief to our shelter. But if he was a dog person, he couldn't be all that bad. "What would you show an art novice on her first time here?"

His face lit up. "I thought you'd never ask."

"Margaret says you're an artist." I realized even if Henry gave me clues about something related to the theft, I'd have no idea. But maybe after his tutorial, things would make more sense on Saturday.

When I had a chance to compare notes with Persephone.

"I am, but I don't worry about making my art commercial. So it's taken a backseat to teaching."

"What makes art commercial?" I asked. The reward money would go a long way for him. Stolen art would supplement that schoolteacher's salary, too.

"Usually it's approachable, agreeable, people want to see it in their house. Art should challenge everything you believe and make you think differently."

"I saw some of your work the other night when I met Margaret. I liked it." It took me a while to come to that conclusion, but I was still thinking about it, which had to mean something.

"Margaret's been my biggest cheerleader since I moved to Boston. I might have given up on sculpting altogether if it hadn't been for her encouragement."

We entered the exhibit area. I'd done a little online research about the artist. He'd been a protégé of Bournaise. They'd inhabited an artist colony in a remote, coastal area of France, and their work had been called groundbreaking and important, but my untrained eye didn't quite see why.

"Margaret said she was Bellamy Bournaise's muse." I hoped I didn't divulge a secret.

Henry grinned. "That woman is a lot more powerful than people give her credit for."

"How so?" I asked too loudly. Other patrons who came to take in the exhibit were side eyeing me. Brooke and Casey were in the room too, and I winced as Casey reached out and touched a boxy exhibit made of straight pins. The docents scolded her as she backed away.

Henry saw it, too. He pressed his lips together as she left the room. "That's what's cool about this exhibit. It has the power to make people forget they're in a museum and make them want to interact with it."

"True." I was relieved he didn't find Brooke's faux pas too cringeworthy. "You didn't answer my question about Margaret. How is she powerful?"

"She knows how to speak the artists' language. She's smart and knows good work, important work, when she sees it. She makes suggestions that take a piece from good to great."

The woman I'd met seemed kind but understandably frazzled, considering the circumstances. And there was something about her that I connected with: people underestimated her. "Why did she leave France after Bellamy died?"

"She wanted a change of scenery, to reconnect with her family after years away. It hasn't been easy for her, and after the theft, I wouldn't be surprised if she decided to sell the house and go back to France.

But it would be a huge loss for the local art community."

So he didn't want her to go, but he thought the theft might drive her away. I liked Henry, which seemed dangerous. I had to stay objective.

We wandered around the exhibit. The work definitely wasn't commercial, by Henry's definition. It gave me a lot to think about. Henry explained the similarities between this and Bournaise's work with ease that made me understand. He must be a great teacher.

"Margaret said she didn't want to sell Bellamy's work. Why did she change her mind?"

"The time's right. Bournaise is having a moment, and she lived these paintings. I see it both ways—they're the only living, breathing part of his memory she has left, and at the same time, it might feel good to let go. But I think her niece pressured her to act before she was ready."

"She seems concerned with the bottom line."

"You met her?"

I nodded.

He tensed. "Some people love beauty. Others love money."

"That's a pretty good way to describe her, from what I can tell." I sighed. "I never understood people who loved money."

Henry furrowed his brow.

"When I was younger, everyone encouraged me to go into business. They said I'd never make money doing anything else. I'm terrible with numbers, and I don't have a competitive bone in my body. I listened, because I was a kid and what did I know? After college, I got a job at a brokerage house."

A corner of his lip turned up into a smile. "How'd that go?"

"I got fired. It was a mercy killing, to be honest." I was probably saying way too much.

"That's why I want to expose my students to as much art as possible. To show them how many ideas are actually out there, and how badly we need theirs."

We were back in the lobby. Brooke and Casey were sitting at the café with fancy-looking drinks and a dessert plate between them. "I've worked at the shelter ever since."

"What did you want to do?"

"I wanted to become a veterinarian." I still toyed with the idea of going back to school. "But I'm still helping animals."

"It's important work." He committed to the smile, but he didn't make eye contact. "There's a place down the street that has great lobster rolls. Just a food truck, nothing fancy. Are you hungry?"

My stomach rumbled, and I darted my gaze

toward my wing women. They were laughing over something and not paying any attention to me, which meant they'd deemed Henry the Hottie safe.

But had I?

# CHAPTER SIX

"These are amazing." I would've totally passed by the truck Henry had ordered the lobster rolls from. We sat on a concrete wall under a multicolored sunset. Ocean waves crashed against it, and seagulls squawked overhead, angling for an opportunity for a French fry.

I listened to their cries, hoping that I'd understand something. I wished I could talk to every animal. Maybe Persephone could teach me how. But I'd probably never see her again after Saturday night. I might never know what happened to Margaret, or the painting.

Or Henry.

All these people had been in my life for less than a week, but somehow, they'd managed to send me down a different path.

Nothing from the seagulls. But I'd still leave them some fries.

Henry wiped his mouth with his napkin. "This is one of my favorite places. You can see so many different parts of the city from here. The airport, and the shipping ports. Makes me feel like I've gone somewhere without leaving the city."

"Do you know anything about Margaret's cat?" I groaned inwardly. So smooth.

He furrowed his brow at my change of subject as he swallowed a bite of his lobster roll. "She's a cat."

"Of course she is." I couldn't stop this train now that it was in motion. I needed to own my weird. It wasn't like this was a date, and I was trying to impress Henry. "Have you picked up on anything unusual about her?"

He shrugged. "She likes to sleep in the front window of the gallery. It's the sunniest spot in the room. Gotta respect that."

"So nothing unusual."

Another funny look. "Margaret baby talks to her, which is funny, because it's so unlike Margaret. And the cat seems to hate it."

She did, but I couldn't tell him that. "I'm wondering how she wound up in my shelter in New Hampshire. Doesn't seem to fit with the theft."

His gaze shifted to the shipping containers on the

horizon. Seagulls still cawed around us, but there was something peaceful about Henry, like he was the calm in the middle of the storm. "The two things might not be related."

But they were. "Do you have any ideas who could've done it? Are there other people who spend a lot of time at the gallery? Anyone who showed an unusual interest in the painting?"

He paused for a moment and shook his head. "I'm mostly there late in the afternoon, because of my school schedule, and after hours. So it was often just Margaret and me, and sometimes her handyman."

"Sully?"

He grinned. "That guy's a trip. He's always up in arms over what he hears on sports radio. I've had to talk him off the ledge more than once."

My heart knocked so hard against my ribcage there was no way Henry wouldn't sense my apprehension. "Are the two of you friends?"

"Not beyond the gallery. He cracks me up. Margaret swears he can fix anything."

"Is he interested in the paintings at all?"

"I'm not even sure he's noticed them."

I took another bite of my lobster roll. I usually ate all the lobster first and then the bun, but I was trying to be classy. "How did you connect with Margaret?

"I heard that Bellamy Bournaise's partner opened a gallery in Boston and I went and introduced myself. We have people in common, and I've been helping her come up with ways to capitalize on the foot traffic she gets from tourists."

"Did Margaret ever express concern over anyone who came into the gallery?"

"I've already talked to the police, Addie." He gave me a tight smile.

"Sorry. I didn't mean it to come out that way." The truth was, I liked Henry. Even if I shouldn't. I might never have swiped right on his picture—okay, that was a lie, but I probably would've chickened out if this was an actual date—and I'd become an unexpected part of the theft. There wasn't exactly etiquette for this situation.

"I bet you're a great teacher. You did an amazing job of explaining the exhibit to me."

His lips quirked into a smile. "You asked great questions."

"Guess questions are kind of my thing." I bit into a fry. "I can't stop thinking about how me winding up with Persephone and someone taking the painting could be connected. If Margaret owns that house and she's sitting on all those Bournaises, she's got some money. Do you think they could be extorting her?"

"Like an art dealer."

"Or a real estate agent."

"Not that she mentioned. She got annoyed with the dealers and their lowball offers. She'd send them packing. It was a thing of beauty."

"Sorry I didn't get to see it." I could totally picture it.

"Bournaises are going for crazy money right now. I wouldn't be surprised if that painting has already changed hands." He rubbed his face with his hand and sighed.

"Would any of those people have access to the gallery after hours? The police don't seem to be taking the break-in seriously because there's no sign of forced entry."

"I never saw anyone else there after hours."

"Does Margaret ever forget to lock up?"

He shook his head. "There's a code on the keypad. It automatically disarms the security system."

"So whoever did this was able to get in quietly while Margaret was upstairs and take off with the painting and the cat."

He put the food containers into the paper bag. "I could ask how you wound up with her cat and why you're so concerned with finding who did this."

I opened my mouth, about to lay into him with a hearty dose of *how dare you*. But of course he thought I was suspicious. That was probably why he'd invited me out tonight. "Persephone was left in a duct-taped box on my doorstep in the middle of the night. We often reunite lost animals with their owners and stay in touch after the adoption to make sure everything goes smoothly. If something else happens and Persephone's involved, she might not be so lucky next time."

"That makes sense," he said quietly, and his gaze was focused on the ocean. "I feel that way about my students. Sometimes there's only so much I can do to help them, even when I know they need more from me. I'm an art teacher. It sounds so insignificant, but I might be the last chance of stopping these kids from making a bad decision."

"What made you call me at the shelter?"

"Margaret raved about you. She was impressed that you went the extra mile to reunite her with her cat. She thought there was more to you than met the eye. And I do, too."

It shouldn't have felt like a compliment. Henry could be dangerous. "I'd never heard of Galerie Bellamy until Persephone...until I saw the story online."

"I don't want to end this night on a sour note," he said. "It sounds like we both want to see Margaret get the painting back."

I managed a smile. "We do."

"Tell me more about the shelter."

"Thank you for asking. No one ever does."

He furrowed his brow. "Why not?"

"Probably because they'd rather forget the unpleasantries—that some animals come to us in bad shape. We're a no-kill shelter, and we do our best to make sure everyone feels like they have a home. Every single day is different. It's not an easy job, but there's nothing I'd rather do."

"What else do you like to do?"

I laughed, thinking of Brooke and Casey. "I order takeout and watch cooking shows."

"Do you like to cook?"

"I believe in leaving such things to the experts."

"Will you be at the party on Saturday night?"

"I will."

He grinned. "Me too."

Brooke and Casey were in front of the food truck, gesturing madly at me. I couldn't figure out what they were trying to say without blowing our cover.

"We start early at the shelter." I stretched and tried to make sly eye contact with my friends, to stop them before they made a scene. "And it's a long drive back."

"Yeah, I have an early start too." He pulled out his phone and swiped. "I need to get a ride. With the T strike, things are crazy in the city."

I bundled up my trash and sprinkled the rest of my fries on the rocks below. The seagulls dive-bombed in appreciation.

"Do you come to the city often?" he asked as we walked back.

"Almost never."

"Sounds like that's changing if you're coming back on Saturday."

Brooke and Casey were right behind us, close enough to hear our conversation. I stopped in front of our parking lot, and I hoped they were paying attention so they didn't bump into us. "This is where I'm parked."

He turned to me. "Maybe you'd like to go to a Sox game sometime?"

I raised a brow. "You can get tickets?" Every game was sold out and they went for a fortune on the secondary market.

"My uncle's had season tickets since I was a kid. He can't go to as many games anymore, and he lets me pick a few games. If you'd like to come with me, let me know."

"I'd love that."

"I had fun tonight, Addie." He gave me a crooked grin. "We can compare notes on our investigations on Saturday."

Brooke and Casey were sitting in the car, waiting for me.

I might have watched him walk back to the museum for a little too long, judging from the beep of the horn.

"I totally thought he was going to kiss you," Brooke said when I climbed into the back seat.

Casey turned around and gave me the same look she usually reserved for the dogs when they peed on the floor. "You can't just leave the museum like that, Addie. We were totally freaked out when we couldn't find you."

"He's harmless, I think."

"You also think he stole a priceless painting," Brooke reminded me as a blush crept up my face. "That doesn't change because Henry turned out to be a hottie. Did you get any good information out of him?"

"Not really. He said there were art brokers hanging around because Bournaise is hot, and I know Margaret's on the fence about selling. And that she's received offers for the house. But none of those people would have the security code."

"Maybe a delivery person looking to make a quick buck when they realized the old woman is sitting on a goldmine?" Casey offered.

"Wouldn't they deliver during business hours?"

"True." Brooke tapped her finger against her lips as we sat in traffic. "Could it be some sort of hacker? Or someone who figured out the code from watching other people use it? Or maybe she left it on a sticky note somewhere?"

I shrugged.

"It would be so cool if we figured this out. Maybe we could open a side hustle as a private investigation firm." Casey laughed. "We save animals and solve crimes."

"Think about how amazing that would look on our dating profiles," Brooke said. "And my postgrad applications."

"I don't think this will be a regular thing, but maybe we can use some of our new detective skills to find lost pets' parents, especially if Casey keeps touching art exhibits."

"I thought we were going to get tossed out." Brooke laughed.

Casey's face reddened. "It was made of straight pins. It was so...touchable."

"Do you think he did it?" Brooke asked.

"We both managed to accuse each other of taking the painting."

She gasped. "How did he think *you* did it?"

"He thinks it's suspicious that I wound up with Persephone." As we drove away from the museum, it gave me perspective. "He's definitely got motive. The money. He's got access with the code. He's friendly with the handyman, who seems like he'd be able to do the heavy lifting. But he has a lot of respect for Margaret and the paintings. It will be interesting to see the two of them interact at the party."

Casey turned around in her seat. "Did you tell him about Persephone?"

"That I could talk to her?"

She nodded.

"I hinted around, trying to ask him if he could talk to her without actually asking him, and wound up making it sound like I thought he'd taken the painting."

"So how did you leave it with him?"

"He asked me to a Red Sox game."

"That's a date, Addie."

"Yeah, it probably is."

We were stopped in traffic, and Henry was in the next car. He turned and met my gaze, his face lighting up as he waved.

Brooke smiled at me in the rear-view mirror. "Sounds like you might get a reward out of this no matter what."

# CHAPTER SEVEN

Casey and Brooke thought I should get lucky. Or at least, wear Lucky. They'd brought the contents of their entire closets to Helping Paws, but the LBD was the clear winner.

"We should come with you." Brooke frowned and walked around me in a circle, tapping her finger against her chin as Casey draped a scarf around my neck. The only thing harder than finding out who took the Bournaise was making me feel comfortable in this dangerously low-cut dress. It was a far cry from my usual big T-shirts and leggings. "Maybe Persephone can talk to us, too. She could have a connection with shelter workers."

"You would've heard her when she was here. She's not exactly shy."

"We didn't get to spend any time with her before you brought her back to Margaret," Casey countered.

"The party is invite-only. I wish I could bring you. Going to a party where I don't know anyone is like one of those dreams where you show up at work naked."

"You know Henry."

"Right. But he's probably got connections in the art world, and he won't want to have a clueless barnacle stuck to him."

"He did ask you on another date." Casey waggled her eyebrows. "Isn't the point of this party to sell paintings? I'd think she'd want as many people there as possible."

"Margaret wanted to cancel. She's not sure she wants to sell any of the paintings anymore."

"What if it's an inside job? Margaret pretended the painting was stolen so she doesn't have to sell it?" Brooke handed me a long necklace. "Loop this around your neck. You won't be so self-conscious about your cleavage all night."

I groaned and sat down, tugging at the hem of the dress. I wasn't ready for Lucky. I must have a pair of nice black pants and a dressy shirt in my closet that still fit. "She's still mourning Bellamy. This can't be easy for her."

"But the cat," Brooke said. "If she packed her up

in that awful box and just left her here…Ugh. Make sure you bring her home with you."

"She loves her cat." So there went that theory. "Maybe I should just leave well enough alone. I did my job. I reunited Persephone with her owner."

"Can Persephone talk to Margaret?" Casey asked.

"No. She seemed flabbergasted by my claim and we never had a chance to talk about it."

"You can't abandon Persephone." Brooke picked up one of the cats we'd let out of the kennel for the afternoon. We liked to give the animals as much freedom as we could. It kept them social, and prospective adopters loved seeing them free. "Imagine if you found the only person you could communicate with, and then, just like that, you never saw them again."

"Not sure Margaret's looking to do joint custody."

Casey sat next to me, and another cat jumped into her lap. "What would you do with the reward money?"

"Put it into the shelter. Persephone says these kitties have a taste for tuna. Maybe buy a few outfits so I don't have to keep borrowing your clothes when I want to look nice."

"For your dates." Brooke grinned.

"For whatever."

"So you're doing this for Persephone, and all our

animals. You can't let them down. You have to go tonight," Casey said.

"You don't want to let Henry down, either." Brooke waggled her brows at me.

"No. I'm hoping that maybe Sully will be there too."

"Wait, who? Did you go on another date without telling us?"

"No." I laughed. "He's Margaret's handyman. I tried to get him to come fix something here but he wouldn't come out this far." I thought he might have been the one to bring Persephone here, but he'd acted like New Hampshire was closer to Mars than Boston, and I scratched that possibility off the list. "It's a long shot, because everyone says he's not into art, but I feel like he'd have a unique perspective."

"I have a feeling I'll be starving by the time we're done getting everyone settled for the night. If Brooke and I were to say, have dinner in the Back Bay, would you like a ride to the party?" Casey proposed.

"That way you won't get nervous when it takes forever to get there and park because of the strike, so you can be relaxed when you're looking for clues. And when we're done, we can do a little window shopping. Something tells me things look different from the other side of the glass."

"You'll never get a reservation for a Saturday night."

"We can eat at the bar."

"Fine, you can come." I let my head fall back in defeat and the ladies high-fived.

"When this is over, you have to promise to wear some of those new clothes out with us," Brooke said. "There's never a dull moment with you, Addie."

"First time I've ever heard that."

"Stop underestimating yourself," she said. "You always tell us how boring and awkward you are, but you're about to solve a major art heist and you might have scored Henry the Hottie in the process."

"When you put it that way, I do sound pretty awesome." I laughed.

"I finally worked on my course last night, and I plan to ask my students to make a list of everything they do well or enjoy doing, even if they're awful at it. You need to do that, Addie. You do amazing things for the animals at Helping Paws, and you gave us jobs. We were nervous too, but you made us believe in ourselves. That's talent. And what if Persephone's not the only cat you can talk to?"

"I'd love to get her back in here to talk to some of our residents to see what we're missing." I scratched the head of the kitty in Casey's lap. I was rewarded with an audible purr. But no words. "It might help us place more of the animals, or at least make cuter, more accurate adoption ads for them."

Brooke and Casey had started making social media posts that looked like dating profiles for our animals, and adoption requests skyrocketed. The problem was, once we placed an animal, there was always someone else who needed that kennel. Especially in a no-kill shelter.

"I'll talk to Margaret."

"Are you sure this is invite-only?" Brooke whistled as our car crawled past the gallery while she looked for a place to park. "There's a line to get in."

"I thought if we came early, I'd have a chance to talk to Persephone and come up with a plan before the rest of the guests arrived." My heart sank. Now I'd have to get creative.

"Maybe we can run interference for you. Our reservations aren't until eight-thirty." Casey considered the line as she waited for the light to change. "We can come in like clueless tourists and make a lowball offer on one of the featured paintings. The patrons will be aghast, and no one will notice you're talking to a cat."

"I'll text you if I need you." But I had to be

honest with myself—all possibilities were on the table tonight. The ladies might be my secret weapon after all. "I can get out here."

"Are you sure?" Brooke asked.

"I'm wearing a dress called Lucky and co-conspiring with a cat. I've never been surer of anything in my life." I took a deep breath and gripped the door handle. "Don't do anything I wouldn't do tonight, ladies."

Casey rolled down the window and called after me. "Stop underestimating yourself, Addie. You've got this."

# CHAPTER EIGHT

Margaret and Nicole opened the doors minutes after I got in line.

"I'm so glad you came." Margaret kissed me on the cheek. "I wasn't sure we'd see you tonight."

"I'm excited to see Bellamy's work."

"We scaled back," Nicole said. From her frown, she wasn't as happy to see me as her aunt. "The tone of the exhibit changed without its centerpiece, and coming up with a new message on the fly is challenging."

"I didn't realize you were so involved in the presentation of the exhibit." The last time I'd spoken to her, she sounded more interested in her aunt's safety than the work.

She waved her hand dismissively. "I'm not. But I want to make sure this isn't too stressful for my aunt."

"You underestimate her."

"You don't know me or my family," Nicole gasped. Margaret turned away from the gentleman she'd been talking to.

"I'm sorry." My apology was for Margaret, not her niece. Nicole got under my skin, giving me flashbacks to the brokerage firm, the middle management that always made me feel like a total hot mess.

She rolled her eyes and accepted a drink off the waiter's tray before turning away from me. Her hand was on the arm of an older man, and she laughed too loudly. Great. I'd already managed to cause a scene in the first minute of the party.

Maybe the girls were still stuck in traffic on this street...they could come save me after all.

"Don't worry about her," Margaret said. "She means well, but she doesn't understand people like us."

I breathed a sigh of relief. Margaret was cool and sophisticated in her patterned wrap dress, knee-high boots, and straight gray hair that shined like glass, and even though I looked great in Lucky, I worried I smelled like cat pee.

"What do you mean by people like us?"

"The ones that march to the beat of their own

drum." She gave me a knowing smile and pulled me away from the crowd. I scanned the room, looking for Persephone. The cat didn't give off vibes like she'd be the type to hide under the furniture in a room full of strangers. I expected her to be perched on top of one of the exhibits, daring the patrons to admire her more than the art.

"Did Henry call you?" she asked in a low voice.

"He did." My heart thumped at the mention of his name.

"I hope you don't mind I gave him your number. He's a bit of a lost soul. I thought maybe the two of you would hit it off."

I hadn't heard from him since our night out, so he might have been reconsidering his offer of the baseball game. "We went to the ICA, and he introduced me to Bellamy's friend's exhibit. After this week, I'll be an art expert."

"All you need to know about art is that it expresses emotions that words can't do justice." She smiled at someone who came into the gallery, and I had a feeling my time with her was about to end for the night. "It should make you ask questions and dig deeper. You might never find the answer you're looking for, but you'll learn so much more than you ever expected. Not many are willing to go on that journey. Now, if you'll excuse me."

There was a message in there. I accepted an hors d'oeuvres from the tray and popped it into my mouth as I scanned the room. I'd come into the night still wondering if Henry might know something about the theft or if there was an overzealous art dealer looking to cut out the middleman, but I had to consider that Margaret had wanted to keep Bellamy's paintings for herself.

She moved through the crowded room with ease. She was all about the art, and even though she had no problems talking to anyone here, they weren't her people. She was cooler than them, more cultured, and from the undertones of what Nicole and Henry had said, probably had more money than everyone here— especially if she was sitting on the goldmine of Bellamy's work.

Somehow I'd wound up in the corner, with multiple hors d'oeuvres napkins balled in my hand giving tight smiles to anyone who looked in my general direction.

Awkward.

I had to find Persephone.

Even more awkward.

I squeezed through the crowd, apologizing as I bumped into people.

"Addie," Henry called to me. He was standing with Nicole. Maybe it was the champagne, but she'd definitely changed her tune toward him when he was in front of her. He'd worn a suit tonight. His hair curled around his ears, and he pushed his glasses up his nose as he smiled at me.

Nicole glared at me. Whatever.

"Hi. I was hoping I'd see you here tonight."

"Likewise."

"I'll leave the two of you alone." Nicole turned on her heel.

"She does not like me," I said.

"She doesn't like any of us." He laughed. "She sees this gallery as a nuisance and as a place she can cash in. When she doesn't get what she wants, she projects it onto Margaret not being able to handle it."

Interesting. I wasn't sure I could trust Henry yet, so I had to be careful with my words. He could be baiting me. As much as Margaret thought I had a place in this world, it was completely unfamiliar to me, and I was definitely the outsider. "Margaret can totally handle it."

He nodded. "She's not a woman to be underestimated. She'll have these art dealers eating out of her hand by the end of the night. The walls will be bare."

So much for thinking they were taking advantage of her. "How do you know which ones are the art dealers?"

"They're the ones on their phones, talking to the

houses they work for, trying to figure out what they can offer. There will be bidding wars for a couple of these pieces."

"What kind of money will they go for?"

He shrugged. "Six figures, probably. Maybe seven."

My mouth dropped. "Who can spend that kind of money on a painting?" My voice was too loud, and a few partygoers turned and gave me a look. The same one Nicole had shot in my direction.

At the shelter, a shoestring budget felt like a luxury.

"Not many. They're investors, people looking to put their money in something other than the stock market." His eyes scanned the room. "Most of the people are here looking for connections of other kinds. They don't care about the art."

"That bothers you."

His shoulders tensed under his suit. "It does. Bournaise's work has a message, and these people don't care enough to actually look at the paintings long enough to see what he was trying to tell them. It's a waste. I told Margaret this was the wrong place for her gallery, but this house has been in her family for generations, and it makes sense to her."

"I guess everyone here has their own agenda." And time was slipping away from me. This could be my only chance to figure out who'd stolen the painting. I had a feeling they were in this room. If they could get into the gallery without alarming Margaret in the middle of the night, chances were they'd smiled at her and kissed her on the cheek tonight as everyone around them whispered about the scandal. "Is Sully here?"

"Do you see anyone wearing a backward baseball cap and cargo shorts?"

"No." I laughed. "Excuse me."

I had to find Persephone.

# CHAPTER NINE

The partygoers gave me funny looks as I crouched down and looked under the furniture. Whatever. I'd probably never see any of these people again.

No sign of Persephone.

Brooke and Casey waved at me from outside the window. I cringed, because I could tell they were up to something. Casey nudged Brooke, and they walked in the front door.

"What are you doing?" I whispered between gritted teeth.

"Have you figured it out yet?" Brooke asked. "We saw you talking to Henry."

I groaned and looked around to make sure no one was paying attention to me or the party-crashers. "He's still on my list."

The ladies gave each other a knowing look. "Anyone else?"

My heart pounded. "Look at the room. It's packed, and those people on the phone are dealers. They could potentially spend over a million dollars on a piece tonight."

Brooke whistled. "This room is full of sugar daddies. If I play my cards right, I could kiss my student loan debt goodbye."

"It could be. If the two of you want to mingle..." And just like that, they'd successfully crashed the party. "Make sure you have your story straight about why you're here. And whatever you do, don't mention my name."

I needed to get away from the crowd for a minute and regroup. I breathed a sigh of relief when I reached the hallway, and only found a few servers assembling new trays of treats in the kitchen.

And Persephone hanging out of one of the stools.

"There you are." I took the stool next to her and roughed her fur. "I've been looking for you all night."

One of the servers looked over her shoulder, like I could've been talking to her, but I shrugged her off and turned to the cat.

"That crowd is too much." Persephone's muscles tensed under my touch. "If I stay in here, I can steal shrimp off the tray when no one's looking."

My kind of cat.

"How are they too much for you?"

Another look from the server that I totally ignored.

"All the scents are overwhelming. Perfume and cologne and bad food."

"Do any of them smell like the people who took the painting?"

"Can't tell. Too much going out there, and there's shrimp in here." Persephone had her priorities sorted.

"What did the thieves smell like?" She'd told me before, but I wanted to make sure she said the same thing twice. Or else she could be leading me in the wrong direction.

"Dead flowers."

Same thing. "Have you smelled it in the gallery before?"

I could swear she wrinkled her nose. "All the time."

"Are they here now?"

"Yes."

My heartbeat sped up. We were in the same room with a criminal. Margaret lived here. Nicole had been here every time I'd been here, but that didn't mean that she was here all the time. I had a feeling she was only interested in her aunt when it served her. And

Henry had admitted to being here all the time and to having the door code.

He didn't smell like flowers. He smelled like mint and vanilla, and I could not get distracted thinking about how good Henry smelled.

And he didn't have a car. Persephone had said she'd lost the thieves when they got into a car. I peeked down the hallway to make sure the servers were busy with full trays, and then opened the back door. A light flashed, but there was no audible alarm.

No one came running, so I poked my head out the door. The alleyway was narrow, and a black luxury SUV was parked at the very end of it. Otherwise, there were only the backdoors of the other buildings that shared the alley.

The SUV could've belonged to Margaret. It was as sleek and classy as she was.

Or someone was planning another heist right under all our noses.

I grabbed a shrimp off the tray and gave it to Persephone.

"Thank you." She purred in appreciation.

"Anytime." I patted her again as she worked on her treat. This cat didn't have trust issues. "What does Margaret smell like?"

"Treats." Persephone licked her lips after finishing the last of the shrimp. "You do too. That was how I knew you were going to take care of me. Anyone who smells like that is a good person."

"The treats that were in the box" —which was actually catnip—"Are those your favorites?"

Her eyes brightened. "They were. I was so hungry I was ready to start hunting mice. I'm old now, and they're faster than me. But when I found the treat, I'm a little ashamed to admit I would've eaten anything at that point. When I woke up, I was stuck inside the box until you freed me."

They lured her with something they knew she couldn't refuse. "What did you smell when you woke up?"

"Chemicals. Dead stuff. I picked up some dreadful things on my paws wondering around the city."

"Any more flowers?"

"Maybe."

I stroked Persephone's back as I thought about it. I was pretty sure I had my culprit. Now I just had to figure out how to tell Margaret I'd figured it out. And make her not turn on me in the process.

"Can you handle it by yourself? I'll start the car." A voice in the hallway startled me.

Persephone rose, body stiff. "That's the smell. The person who took the painting is coming."

# CHAPTER TEN

Nicole's face fell when she saw me. But the shock didn't last. She pushed her shoulders back and gave me her familiar scowl. "What are you doing back here?"

"Taking a minute away from the crowd." I looked past her, to the older man she'd left me to talk to earlier tonight. He huffed, his arms full with a sculpture that had to weigh a ton. "Didn't think you were supposed to touch the art exhibits, much less bring them out the back door."

"I'll have you know this man bought this piece." She stepped toward me. It took everything I had not to back up. I knew very little about art exhibits, but after watching the docents descend on Casey for touching the block of straight pins at the ICA, I was pretty sure this was not the way a priceless work of art should be handled. "Now, if you'll get out of our way, he'll be able to put it into his car and we'll be able to enjoy the rest of our evening."

Something wasn't right about this. "Shouldn't he go out the front door?"

Nicole mashed her lips together, nostrils flaring. "He's parked back here."

"There's no one parked back here, Nicole." It was my turn to take a step toward her. I'd caught her off guard enough that she backed up. "Is this what you did the night you stole the painting?"

"You think I stole the painting?" She laughed. "Oh, that's rich. The country bumpkin who's covered in cat hair thinks I'd steal a priceless painting from my own aunt. Go back to New Hampshire, Addie. Leave the investigation to the professionals. You're making a fool out of yourself."

"I know you stole the painting."

A waitress entered the room and backed down the hallway when she saw the scene playing out.

"Get Margaret," I said before she got too far away. "Bring her back here."

"Wh-Who's Margaret?" she asked.

"The person who hired you."

Nicole laughed. "I hired the help. I wouldn't trouble my aunt with such a menial task. She's seventy years old. She doesn't have to work for a living anymore."

I tensed at the way she said work, like it was beneath her. It wasn't bad enough that she'd stolen from her own family, but she didn't need this painting, or the money that its sale on the black market could generate.

"Get the really well put-together lady with straight gray hair, wearing a green patterned dress and black boots." Margaret would stand out in any crowd.

"You really think my aunt is going to take the word of someone she just met over her own family? You're probably the one who stole her cat, looking to cash in on an art theft."

I bristled. Now I knew where Henry got that theory from. "She'll be really disappointed in you."

"I don't care what she thinks, Addie. I'm an adult. Maybe you should try acting like one."

"Stop underestimating her."

Another nostril flare. Nicole did not like being called out. "Who told you I did that? Your new boyfriend, the art lover?"

"He didn't have to."

"Maybe you're in on this with him." Nicole scoffed. "You helped him haul the painting out of here in the middle of the night. Never saw you before the painting was missing."

"What on earth is going on here?" Margaret scanned the kitchen, and her gaze landed on the man with the sculpture. "Why do you have that in the kitchen?"

"Because he was about to haul it out the back door," I said.

Margaret gasped.

"She's delusional, Aunt Margaret." Nicole put her hand on the older woman's shoulder. "Martin noticed a chip in the sculpture, and I know that Henry keeps some of his sculpting supplies back here."

"That's not what you told me." My heart was racing. "They said he bought the sculpture, and they were bringing it to his car out here."

Margaret furrowed her brow. "No one's purchased anything yet—"

"That's not true." Nicole's tone had totally changed since her aunt entered the room. "I've conducted a few purchases tonight."

"None of the pieces for sale have prices on them. I'm the only one who knows what they're worth."

"I've gotten you more than a fair price." Nicole smirked.

"Have all your sales gone out the back door?"

"Nicole, what is going on?"

"Can I put this thing down now?" Martin asked. Someone who'd spent more than a house worth of money on a sculpture definitely wouldn't call it a *thing*. He didn't wait for permission and put the piece on the table with a thud that made me wince. I expected shards of plaster to rain down, but priceless art was sturdier than I thought it would be.

"She's the only one who could've taken the painting," I said. "She was able to slip into the gallery undetected. The door flashes when it's opened, but it doesn't make any noise."

"I'm not the only one with the code," she protested. "And you know that, too."

"I just looked out the door to see what could've happened the night of the theft." I probably did look pretty guilty. "Henry has the code, but he doesn't have a car."

"He could've rented one. Or had an accomplice."

"But then how did Persephone wind up in New Hampshire?" I paced in the tiny room. "Would he have laid a trap for her with catnip in a damp alley, taped it up tight, and dumped her outside a shelter?"

Nicole gasped. "How dare you suggest I could do such a thing!"

"I commend you for choosing a no-kill shelter. You must've done your research." I grinned at her. "You didn't really want to hurt the cat, you just wanted to make your aunt feel bad enough that she closed the gallery."

Nicole's lips parted. "How did you know it was my aunt's cat? She wasn't wearing any tags."

She just admitted it. Adrenaline flooded my body, and I was practically seeing stars. "Persephone told me."

She laughed. "The *cat* told you."

I nodded. "She told me the thief was on the way down the hall before you walked in. She says you smell like dead flowers."

"That perfume is awful, Nicole," Margaret added.

"I'll have you know it's very expensive perfume. Not that you would know that." She raked her gaze over me. "In your hand-me-down outfit."

"Borrowed," I corrected. Lucky deserved more respect, because the dress was living up to its name. "How much does your dead flower perfume go for? About as much as a Bournaise?"

"Enough! Both of you." Margaret waved her arms and turned to her niece. "Why would you do such a thing?"

"You're...really believing her? She thinks a cat can talk to her. She's here covering up for Henry."

"Henry was the one who alerted me the sculpture was missing. I was on my way back here when the waitress let me know there was trouble."

"Auntie, I didn't do it."

"Why were you headed out the back door with a

man who's not your husband with a sculpture you didn't pay for?"

Nicole's mouth dropped. "I told you he was going to fix it. He was trying to help you, like I am." She glared at me.

Martin had his hand on the door. I'd been so focused on Nicole I hadn't seen him move across the kitchen.

"Looks like he's trying to leave before the police get here," I said.

Nicole groaned. "There's no need for the police to come. They've completed their investigation."

"I thought maybe I should move the car," he muttered.

"Why was it in the alley in the first place?"

He grunted and walked out the door.

"If he altered the sculpture, he'd render the piece worthless." Margaret shook her head. "Then what would happen when someone tried to buy it, Nicole? It would be considered a fraud and I'd be a laughing-stock. So either you were trying to leave without paying for the sculpture, or ruin it. And if Addie hadn't been back here to stop you, you would've told me it was my fault. That the gallery is too much for me."

"You're stressed."

"Of course I am! My own niece is sabotaging me."

Margaret looked over her shoulder. She'd raised her voice. The party was still in full swing, but soon, people would know what was happening back here.

"Why don't you want your aunt to have the gallery, Nicole?" I asked. "You've mentioned a few times that you think it's too much for her, and you think she should retire. She loves it. Why do you want to take it away from her?"

She let out an exasperated sigh. "Auntie, this house is worth millions. The paintings are popular now, but what happens when Bellamy's fifteen minutes is over? The gallery will be empty, like it was before. You'll lose money, and your retirement won't be comfortable."

"Who said I wanted to retire?"

"If you sold, you could move back to France with your artist friends and the never have to worry about anything again. You know so much about art, but it's not the same as being business savvy."

"I've never cared about such things."

"But don't you want to take care of your family? We've had some bad fortune lately with investments, and selling this property could do a lot of good for all of us."

"So you thought if you drummed up some contro-versy and took the painting, you could sell the inven-tory, and then convince your aunt to sell the house.

And you wanted to convince her she was too old to have the gallery by having the painting stolen and dumping a cat at a shelter. Poor old Margaret can't handle the stress. She can't even keep a cat. Get the old woman out of the way, no reason for her to be attached to Boston or the house, and be set for life."

"That's not what I said at all," Nicole challenged. "I'm taking care of my family."

"So am I." Margaret picked up the receiver of the ancient phone hanging on the wall. "And you can tell the police the rest of the story when they get here."

# CHAPTER ELEVEN

"We missed our dinner reservations," Brooke said. The gallery party was supposed to end at nine, but no one was leaving when the police showed up and dragged Margaret's niece out in handcuffs. Martin was still at large, never coming back after he "moved the car." Rumor had it that she'd been having an affair with the city's biggest real estate developer, and if I had to guess, he had an eye on building on this very spot.

Now, we had a reason to celebrate.

"Good thing, I'm totally stuffed. I'm going to have to spend some serious time on the elliptical tomorrow after all these cheese balls." Casey put her hand on her stomach. "Addie, I can't believe you figured out who stole the painting."

"I can't either. I never thought it could actually be

Nicole, but now it makes so much sense." I was still in shock. The police had questioned me, and I'd told them everything I'd told Margaret. Including that Persephone had talked to me. The officer's eyebrows rose but he'd taken it in stride.

Maybe I wasn't the only one who could talk to animals.

"You thought it was Henry, didn't you?"

I looked over at my new friend. He was standing in front of one of the paintings, waving his hands as he told someone all about it. The same way he had for me at the museum. He noticed me and winked.

"I did. But then I didn't, because he's so passionate about art I can't imagine him ever doing something so disrespectful to a painting. Or to Margaret."

"Do you think you'll go to a Red Sox game with him?" Casey asked.

"You can totally buy your own tickets now, if you want to." Brooke stopped the waiter and got us another round of champagne. "What will you do with the reward money?"

"Margaret hasn't offered it to me yet." She'd mentioned that she might not offer a reward. Or was that Nicole? I certainly wouldn't ask for it. I'd stopped one person from taking advantage of her, and I had no plans of taking Nicole's place. "But if she gives it to me, I'll invest in the shelter."

"What about getting a place of your own? So you don't have to deal with your sister anymore?"

I shrugged. "We'll see."

The crowd was starting to thin, now that the excitement had subsided. Persephone wandered out from the back room and came straight over to us, rubbing against our legs.

"Here's our hero!" Casey cooed as she leaned down to pet Persephone. "I wish I could talk to you too. Something tells me you do more than solve crimes."

"You did good." I roughed the fur on the top of her head.

"You don't know the last of it," Persephone said as I picked her up. "Things got so stressful when the police were back there, I managed to cough up a hairball into Nicole's bag."

"Good girl." That thing would be ripe by the time she finally got the bag back. It was probably being held as evidence.

"I hope you get lots of tuna. Maybe even some lobster." Maybe Henry could let me know the name of that food truck he brought me to...

"Addie, can I talk to you?" Margaret asked.

The police waved to me on their way out the

door. I'd given them my information in case they had any other questions. I didn't expect to hear from them after I told them the smoking gun came from a cat, but I'd do whatever it took to help out Margaret.

"Of course." I followed her to the kitchen, Persephone still in my arms.

She motioned for me to take a seat. "I can't thank you enough for what you did tonight."

"I didn't really do anything. I was in the right place at the right time."

She waved me off. "You took the disappearance of Bellamy's painting seriously when no one else did. Nicole had painted me as a dithering old lady to the police, one who'd left the door open and let anyone who paid attention to me come and go. That was one of the reasons I wanted you to meet Henry. I had a feeling she was going to try to pin this on him and I wanted him to have a solid character witness."

"I told the police Persephone can talk to me. Not sure they'll be interested in what else I have to say."

"There's more to life than what we're told. It's one of the lessons we learn from art." She opened a leather-bound checkbook. "How should I make this out?"

"Make it out to Helping Paws." We'd be able to place so many more pets and rescue others from higher-risk shelters.

A lot of money had passed by me when I worked at the brokerage, but it never felt real. This was more money than I'd ever been paid at once, and it felt awesome.

She shook her head. "I'll make a sizeable donation to the shelter. I want you to spend some of this money on yourself, Addie. You deserve to celebrate. What do you want?"

"I...uh..." It had been so long since I thought about what I wanted. "I'm not sure."

"Maybe we can do an auction once the stolen painting is recovered, and it will go to your shelter." Margaret put her hand over mine. "I was reluctant to let go of the painting because I didn't think anyone could appreciate it more than me. Now I've found a way to put it to good use. Bellamy would be proud."

"He was lucky to have you."

Persephone purred in my lap. "She's a good human."

"He was a wonderful man." Margaret closed her eyes for a long blink, and I had a feeling Bellamy was right here with us in the gallery that bared his name. The gallery that changed my life. "Speaking of being meant for each other, I think you should keep Purry Pants."

"What?" I couldn't have heard her right.

"I adore her, but she has a special bond with you.

You understand each other." Margaret rubbed Persephone's ear. "I bet there's a cat at your shelter that's looking for a little old lady to hang out with and a sunny windowsill to sleep in."

"I might know a few kitties that fit that description." I pulled Persephone away from my chest. "Do you want to come home with me? My tuna budget just drastically improved."

"I'd love to."

"Persephone approves."

"I thought she might," Margaret said. "I have a feeling the two of you might change the world."

Thank you for reading Art Heists and Hairballs! I hope you had fun finding the Bournaise with Addie and Persephone!

Ready for the next adventure? Visit www.baileyboothbooks.com for all the latest news on where Addie and Persephone are headed next! While you're there, sign up for my newsletter—you'll get a free story just for joining.

Wanna hang out?

Facebook: baileyboothbooks

Instagram: baileyboothbooks

# ALSO BY BAILEY BOOTH

**Spy Kitty in the City**

Art Heists and Hairballs

Guard Dogs and Guitars

Kitty Cats and Kitsch

Baseball and Bad Guys

Potluck and Poison

When the Cat's Away box set

www.ingramcontent.com/pod-product-compliance
Lightning Source LLC
Chambersburg PA
CBHW050751160726
48004CB00002B/516